RUMPELSTILTSKIN

Rumpelstiltskin

From the German of the Brothers Grimm

RETOLD & ILLUSTRATED BY

PAUL O. ZELINSKY

PUFFIN BOOKS

For their generous assistance, I would like to thank
Maria Mileaf and Alexandre Proia; and for her support
and forbearance, my wife, Deborah.   P.O.Z.

PUFFIN BOOKS
Published by the Penguin Group
Penguin Books USA Inc., 375 Hudson Street, New York, New York 10014, U.S.A.
Penguin Books Ltd, 27 Wrights Lane, London W8 5TZ, England
Penguin Books Australia Ltd, Ringwood, Victoria, Australia
Penguin Books Canada Ltd, 10 Alcorn Avenue, Toronto, Ontario, Canada M4V 3B2
Penguin Books (N.Z.) Ltd, 182–190 Wairau Road, Auckland 10, New Zealand

Penguin Books Ltd, Registered Offices: Harmondsworth, Middlesex, England

First published in the United States of America by Dutton Children's Books, a division of Penguin Books USA Inc., 1986
Published in Puffin Books, 1996

1 3 5 7 9 10 8 6 4 2

THE LIBRARY OF CONGRESS HAS CATALOGED THE DUTTON CHILDREN'S BOOK EDITION AS FOLLOWS:

Zelinsky, Paul O. Rumpelstiltskin. p. cm.
Summary: A strange little man helps the miller's daughter spin straw into gold for the king on the
condition that she will give him her firstborn child.
ISBN 0-525-44265-0
[1. Fairy tales. 2. Folklore—Germany.] I. Title.
PZ8.Z38Ru 1986 398.2'1'0943 [E] 86-4482

Puffin Books ISBN 0-14-055864-0

Printed in the U.S.A.

This one
is for
Anna

Once there was a poor miller who had a beautiful daughter.

On his way to town one day, the miller encountered the king. Wanting to impress him, the miller said, "I have a daughter who knows the art of spinning straw into gold."

Now, the king had a passion for gold, and such an art intrigued him. So he ordered the miller to send his daughter to the castle straightaway.

When the girl was brought before him, the king led her to a room that was filled with straw. He gave her spools and a spinning wheel, and said, "You may spin all night, but if you have not spun this straw into gold by morning, you will have to die." With that, he locked the door, and the girl was left inside, alone.

There sat the poor miller's daughter, without the slightest idea how anyone could spin straw into gold. For the life of her she did not know what to do. She grew more and more frightened, and then she began to weep.

Suddenly the door sprang open and a tiny man stepped in.

"Good evening, Mistress Miller," he said. "Why are you sob-bing?"

"Oh," the girl cried, "I must spin this straw into gold and I don't know how."

"What will you give me if I spin it for you?" the little man asked.

"My necklace," answered the girl.

The little man took her necklace and sat down at the spinning wheel. He pulled three times—*whir! whir! whir!*—and the spool was wound full of gold thread. He fitted another spool on, and—*whir! whir! whir!*—three pulls and that one too was full. And so it went until morning, when all the straw was spun and all the spools were full of gold.

When the king came at sunrise, he was amazed and delighted,
but all that gold only made him greedier. So he led the miller's

daughter to a larger room filled with straw, and he ordered her to
spin this straw too before dawn, if she valued her life.

The girl did not know what to do. She began to weep. Once more the door opened and the little man stepped in. "What will you give me if I spin this straw into gold for you?" he asked.

"The ring on my finger," answered the girl, and the little man took her ring. Then he set the spinning wheel whirring, and before the night was over, he had spun all the straw into gleaming gold.

Shortly after sunrise, the king returned. Piles of golden spools glowed in the morning light. The king rejoiced at the sight of so much gold, but still he was not satisfied.

He led the miller's daughter to a third, even bigger room that was piled high with straw. "Tonight you must spin this straw too," ordered the king. "And if you succeed, you shall become my wife." Because, he thought, I could not find a richer wife in all the world.

When the king had left, the little man appeared for the third
time. "What will you give me if I spin for you yet once more?" he
asked.

"I have nothing else," the girl replied.

"Then promise that when you become queen, your first child
will belong to me."

The miller's daughter gasped. How could she promise such a thing? Then she thought, But who knows whether that will ever happen? And as she could think of no other way to save herself, she promised, and the little man once again spun all the straw into gold.

When the king came in the morning and found everything as he had wished, he married the miller's beautiful daughter, and she became a queen.

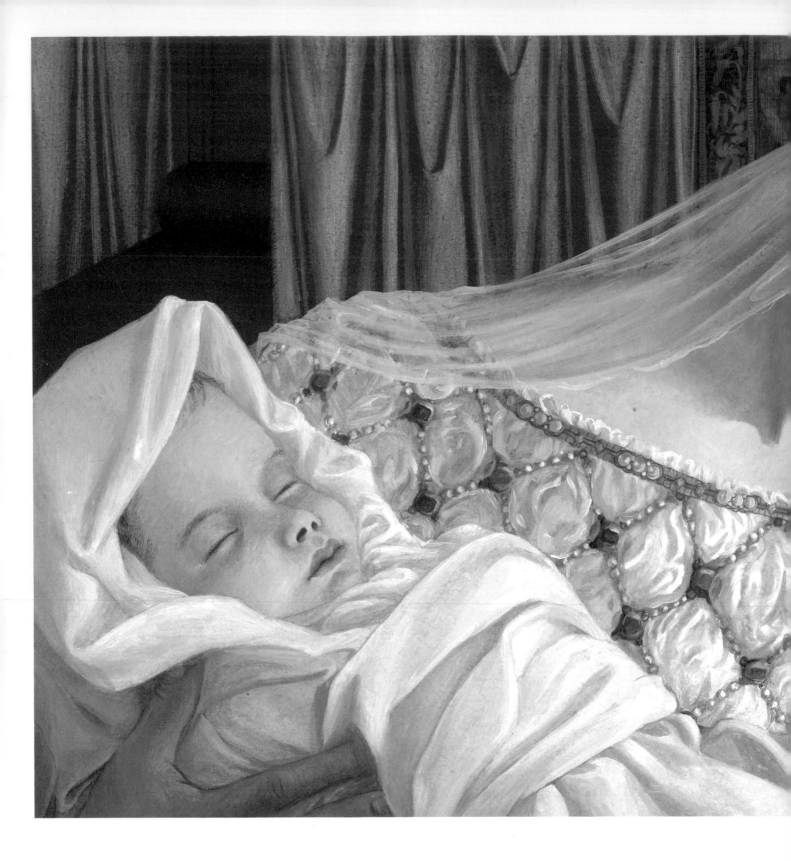

A year passed, and the queen brought a handsome baby boy into the world. She gave scarcely a thought to the little man. But one day he appeared suddenly in her room. "Now give me what you promised me," he demanded.

The queen pleaded with the little man: He could take all the

royal treasure if he would only let her keep her child. But her
pleading was in vain. Then she began to weep so piteously that at
last the little man was moved.

"I will give you three days," he said. "If by the end of that
time you know my name, you may keep your child."

Long into the night the queen sat, and through the next day, thinking over all the names she had ever heard.

That evening the little man returned. Beginning with Caspar, Melchior, and Balthazar, the queen recited every name she knew, one after another. But to each one the little man replied, "That is not my name."

The second day the queen had inquiries made in town, search-
ing for new names. And when the little man came that evening,
she posed the strangest and most unusual ones to him. She tried
Beastyribs and Leg O'Ram and Stringbones—but he would only
reply, "That is not my name."

Now the queen grew truly frightened, and she sent her most
faithful servant into the woods to look for the little man. The

servant searched through thickets and over clearings, deep into the
forest. At last, near the top of a high hill, she spied him.

He was riding on a cooking spoon around a great fire, and crying out:

> I brew my beer, I bake my loaves,
> And soon the queen's own son I'll claim.
> O lucky me! For no one knows
> That Rumpelstiltskin is my name!

The servant made her way back as fast as she could manage and at midday reached the castle. You can imagine how glad the queen was when she heard the name.

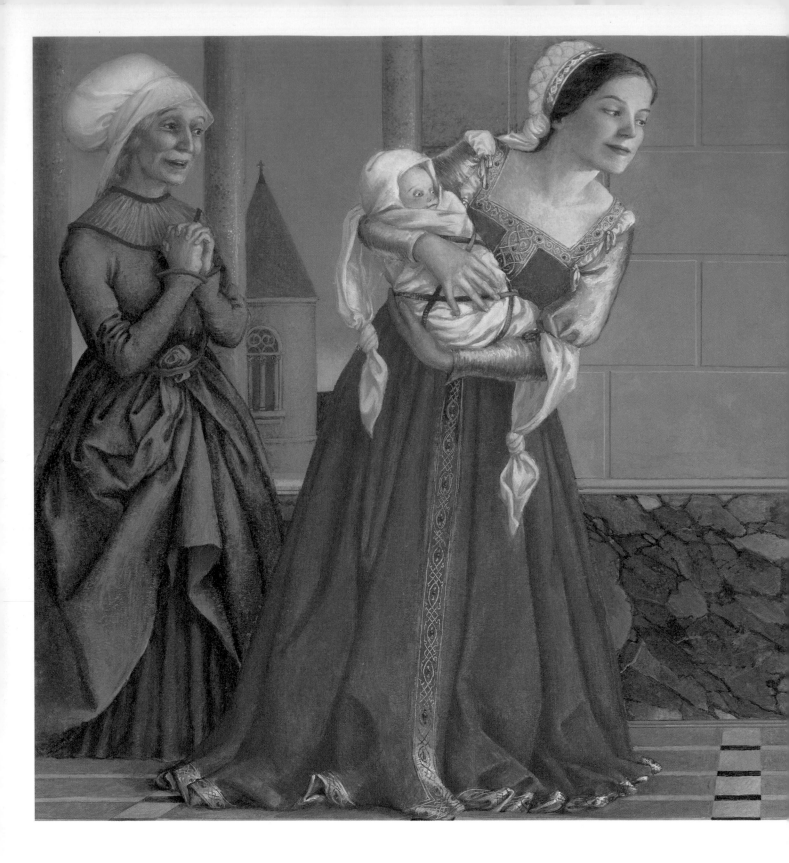

Late that evening the little man arrived. "Now, Mrs. Queen,"
he said, "do you know my name or do I take the child?"
So the queen asked him, "Is your name Will?"
"No."
"Is your name Phil?"

"No."

"In that case, is your name Rumpelstiltskin?"

"The Devil told you that! The Devil told you that!" shrieked Rumpelstiltskin. And in a fury he jumped on his cooking spoon and flew out the window.

And he never was heard from again.

A NOTE ON THE TEXT

Jacob and Wilhelm Grimm began collecting folktales in 1806. Two years later, Jacob sent a story called *"Rumpenstünzchen"* to his friend and former teacher Friedrich Karl Von Savigny. In this story a young girl, given flax to spin into linen, is distressed to find that only gold thread comes out of her spinning wheel. A little man appears and offers to help her by causing a prince to carry her off and marry her. The little man's price, however, is her firstborn child. The princess can keep her child only if she guesses the little man's name. She sends a maidservant into the woods, and the servant sees him riding around his fire on a cooking spoon, chanting his name, *Rumpenstünzchen*. He returns once to let the princess guess his name, and when she does, he flies out the window on his spoon.

"Rumpenstünzchen" was included among the manuscripts the Grimms sent in 1810 to their friend the writer Clemens Brentano. Those manuscripts, most of them direct transcriptions of oral tellings, were later found among Brentano's papers. They constitute the earliest surviving state of what would become, after much extending and amplifying, the

brothers' classic collection, *Children's and Household Tales*, first published in 1812.

This first edition featured a *"Rumpelstilzchen"* ("Rumpelstiltskin") in which a king forces a miller's daughter to turn straw into gold, but there is no mention of spinning or spinning wheels. It is the king who discovers Rumpelstiltskin in the woods, accidently, and happens to tell the queen about it. When the queen guesses Rumpelstiltskin's name, the little man runs off angrily and never comes back.

In the second, 1819, edition of *Children's and Household Tales*, "Rumpelstiltskin" appears in its now most familiar form: The miller's daughter must spin straw into gold; Rumpelstiltskin returns three times for the queen to guess his name; and when Rumpelstiltskin hears his name, he stamps one foot deep into the ground, grabs the other foot, and tears himself in half. The Grimms' notes to that edition state that they compiled this version of the tale "from four versions agreeing in the main, complementary in detail." Those four versions have not survived as separate variants. The 1812 text combined two of them. *"Rumpenstünzchen"* was a fifth variant.

From the third edition of the collection to the last the Grimms published, in 1857, they continued to revise their texts; the alterations on "Rumpelstiltskin" were less substantive than on many of the other tales.

This present text is based principally on the 1819 "Rumpelstiltskin." Some of the dialogue is from later editions, and I have added a few lines where it seemed necessary. I have also diverged in several places to include elements from the earlier versions, hoping to create a text best suited for a picture book.

PAUL O. ZELINSKY